This book belongs to:

ROHIT &

SHREYA.

A catalogue record for this book is available from the British Library

Published by Ladybird Books Ltd
80 Strand London WC2R 0RL
A Penguin Company

2 4 6 8 10 9 7 5 3 1
© LADYBIRD BOOKS LTD MMVI
LADYBIRD and the device of a Ladybird are trademarks of Ladybird Books Ltd

ISBN-13: 978-1-84646-077-7
ISBN-10: 1-84646-077-8

Printed in Italy

Little Red Riding Hood

illustrated by David Parkins

Little Red Riding Hood
lived with her mother
and father in a house
in the forest.

5

One day Little Red Riding Hood's mother said, "Will you take these cakes to Grandmother?"

"Yes," said Little Red Riding Hood, and off she went.

7

Grandmother's house was on the other side of the forest.

And in the forest lived a wolf.

9

When the wolf saw Little
Red Riding Hood he said,
"I will eat her all up!"
And off he ran.

Little Red Riding Hood
knocked on her
grandmother's door.

"Come in," said a
funny voice.

13

Little Red Riding Hood
looked at her grandmother.

"Come closer, my dear,"
said the funny voice.

"Oh, Grandmother," said Little Red Riding Hood. "What big ears you have!"

"All the better to hear you with, my dear," said the funny voice. "Come closer."

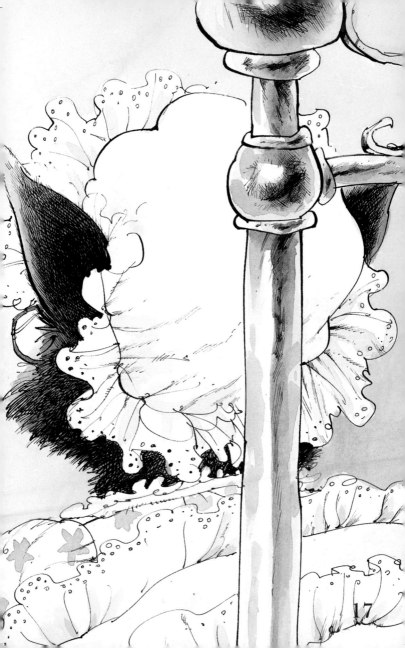

17

"Oh, Grandmother," said Little Red Riding Hood. "What big eyes you have!"

"All the better to see you with, my dear," said the funny voice. "Come closer."

"Oh, Grandmother," said Little Red Riding Hood. "What big teeth you have!"

"All the better to eat you with!" cried the wolf.

21

The wolf jumped up and chased Little Red Riding Hood round and round the house.

"Help!" cried Little Red Riding Hood.

Little Red Riding Hood's father was in the forest. He ran to Grandmother's door with his big axe.

The wolf jumped up when
he saw the axe.
Then he ran and ran
and was never seen in
the forest again.

Read It Yourself is a series of graded readers designed to give young children a confident and successful start to reading.

Level 2 is for children who are familiar with some simple words and can read short sentences. Each story in this level contains frequently repeated phrases which help children to read more fluently. Every page in the story is accompanied by a detailed illustration of the main action, which aids understanding of the text and encourages interest and enjoyment.

About this book

The story is told in a way which uses regular repetition of the main words and phrases. This enables children to recognise the words more and more easily as they progress through the book. An adult can help them to do this by pointing at the first letter of each word, and sometimes making the sound that the letter makes. Children will probably need less help as the story progresses.

Beginner readers need plenty of help and encouragement.